The Mother of Monsters

For Pim,
with love
— F. P.

To my dear
sister Maie
— S. F.

Barefoot Books
2067 Massachusetts Ave
Cambridge, MA 02140

Series Editor: Gina Nuttall
Text copyright © 2011 by Fran Parnell
Illustrations copyright © 2003 & 2011 by Sophie Fatus
The moral rights of Fran Parnell and Sophie Fatus have been asserted

Graphic design by Helen Chapman, West Yorkshire, UK
Reproduction by B&P International, Hong Kong
Printed in China on 100% acid-free paper by Printplus, Ltd
This book was typeset in Chalkduster, Gilligan's Island and Sassoon Primary
The illustrations were prepared in acrylics

Sources:
Hertslet, Jessi. *Bantu Folk Tale*. The African Bookman, Capetown, 1946.

Knappert, Jan, editor and translator. *Bantu Myths and Other Tales*. E. J. Brill, 1977.

ISBN 978-1-84686-560-2

Library of Congress Cataloging-in-Publication Data is
available under LCCN 2011002936

3 5 7 9 8 6 4 2

The Mother of Monsters

A Story from South Africa

Retold by Fran Parnell · Illustrated by Sophie Fatus

Barefoot Books
step inside a story

Contents

CHAPTER 1

The Girl With No Fear

My name is Ntombi.

Long ago in Africa, there lived a young princess called Ntombi. She was the chief's daughter. She was different from the other girls in her tribe. The other girls were quiet and good. Ntombi was not.

She ran everywhere —
jumping, shouting and singing.
She was cheeky and argued
with everyone.

She was always getting
into mischief because she was
not frightened of anything.
Ntombi was a girl with no fear.
She enjoyed wild adventures.

Ntombi's father loved her
dearly. However, he was afraid
that she would get into real
trouble one day. He wanted
Ntombi to live a quiet life. He
wanted her to get married.
Ntombi did not agree.

She just laughed when her
father introduced her to handsome
young princes. "I don't want to
get married," she said.

"I want to see more of the
world and have adventures.
Besides, those princes are no
match for me. I only want to
marry a man who has no fear."

9

For three years, Ntombi's father begged her to get married. For three years, the princess refused. "I want to see the frightening Ilulange River with my own eyes. I will not get married until I have seen it," she said stubbornly.

No, I will not marry!

At first, her father said no. The
river was too dangerous and no one
ever went there. People said that the
Mother of Monsters lived in that river
and she did not like visitors.

But Ntombi begged and
begged her father. In the end,
the chief agreed.

Yippee!

"You may go if you take the
other girls with you," he said.
Ntombi jumped for joy. The other
girls were not so pleased.

This is so scary!

They were frightened, but they loved naughty Ntombi. So, the very next morning, they all set off for the river.

CHAPTER 2

The Dangerous River

The girls climbed up the steep paths. They sang funny songs to hide their fear. Ntombi led them on, skipping and jumping over the high rocks without a care. Then suddenly she stopped.

In front of them the ground dropped away. Far below them there was a terrifying dark space. They had come to a deep, narrow gorge. The steep sides went down, down, down.

They were covered with thick, prickly bushes. The only sound that Ntombi and her friends could hear from below was the noise of a rushing river.

The girls gulped, but
Ntombi's eyes sparkled with
delight. The princess scrambled
down the steep slopes and the
girls followed her. They went
down, down, down to the banks
of the Ilulange River.

The girls looked into the dark water and shivered. But princess Ntombi was disappointed. "So this is the famous river!" she scoffed. "I don't see what is so terrible about it. The water is a little black, but that is probably because the high cliffs above make it look so dark."

Quickly, Ntombi took off
her bracelets and her fancy
skirt. Then she dived into the
cool water. Down, down, down
she went.

"Come and swim!" shouted
Ntombi when she popped up
again.

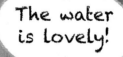
The water
is lovely!

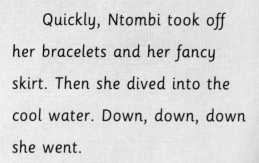

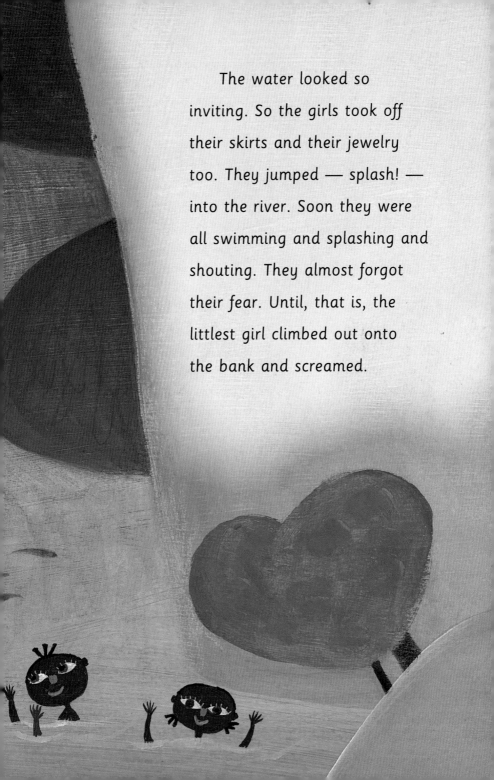

The water looked so
inviting. So the girls took off
their skirts and their jewelry
too. They jumped — splash! —
into the river. Soon they were
all swimming and splashing and
shouting. They almost forgot
their fear. Until, that is, the
littlest girl climbed out onto
the bank and screamed.

"Someone has taken all our
things!" she howled. "It must have
been the Mother of Monsters. Oh,
why ever did we come here?" And
she began to cry.

CHAPTER 3

The Horrible River Monster

Quickly, all the other girls
scrambled out of the river. They ran
to comfort the littlest one.

"Don't cry!" said one of them. "If it
was the Mother of Monsters who took
our things, we should ask her nicely
to give them back. I am sure she will
return them."

The littlest girl turned to face
the river. "Mother of Monsters,
I'm sorry!" she said. "I did not
mean to disturb you. It was
Ntombi's idea to come here!"

In a moment, her clothes and her bracelets came flying out of the river. They landed in a soggy heap on the bank.

One by one, the other girls begged for their clothes back. Each time, the clothes flew up from the dark water and onto the bank.

Finally, only Ntombi was left without her things. But she had a fierce frown on her proud face. She was angry. She said, "Why should a princess have to plead with a river monster? You are a horrible old thing. I am not afraid of you!"

Suddenly a huge head rose out of the water. Two bulging eyes glared down at the princess. Mud poured from the monster's thick, slimy scales.

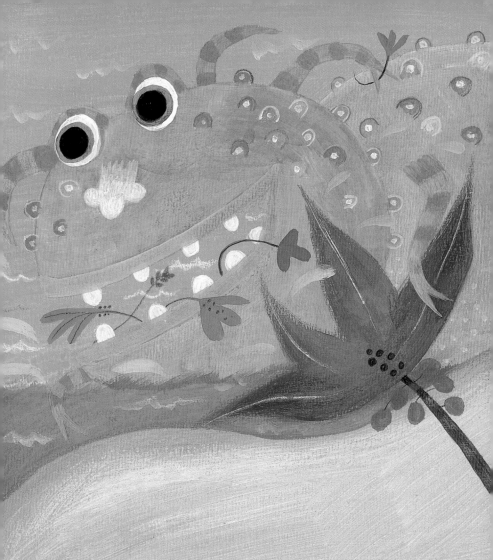

Long green weeds dripped from her
open mouth. Before the princess could
turn and run, the Mother of Monsters
swallowed her in one great gulp.

Ntombi's friends almost
fainted with fright. They
screamed and ran. They
didn't stop running until
they reached home.

CHAPTER 4

The Man With No Fear

When the chief heard
what had happened, he called
for his warriors. He ordered
them to go and rescue the
princess. The warriors were
nervous, but they did as they
were told.

Soon they reached the river
bank. The monster's horrible head
rose up out of the gushing water.
She let out a terrifying roar. Then the
monster swallowed them all whole.

The Mother of Monsters liked
the sweet taste of humans. In fact,
she liked the taste so much that she
climbed right out of the water.

She tramped up the steep sides
of the gorge. She crushed bushes
and trees as she went. The monster
thundered her way across the
countryside, looking for human food.

Everyone ran away as fast as they could, but it was no use.

The monster caught the people in her terrible claws. She ate them up one by one. She smacked her slimy lips as she swallowed them whole.

Mooo!

The more she ate, the hungrier she felt. She gulped down everything that moved. Humans, cattle, dogs and even snarling wild cats all disappeared into her drooling mouth.

Soon she reached a village of huts. A handsome young hunter named Sobabili lived there. His wife had died a few years before, so his children were looking after the cattle.

Quick as a flash, the Mother of Monsters gobbled up the two little children and all the cattle.

Sobabili could hardly believe
his eyes when he came home
from hunting. His home had been
squashed flat by the monster's
bulging belly. His children were
gone. All his cattle were gone.

33

Sobabili was furious, but he was not frightened. He did not fear the monster at all. Sobabili decided to find her. He followed the trail that her belly had left in the ground.

CHAPTER 5

ON the Trail of the Monster

After a while, a wild old elephant came charging towards him. But Sobabili was not afraid. He asked the elephant, "Have you seen the monster that ate my children and ruined my home?"

"Do you mean the Mother of
Monsters, the Crusher of Trees?
Yes, she passed this way. Keep on
going!"

Sobabili thanked the elephant. He
kept going until he saw two young
leopards. They were following him
through the long dry grass. But Sobabili
was not afraid. He asked the leopards,
"Have you seen the monster that ate my
children and ruined my home?"

"Do you mean the Mother of Monsters, the Crusher of Trees, who rose from the river baring her teeth? Yes, she passed this way. Keep on going!"

Sobabili thanked the leopards. He kept going until he saw a roaring lion.

But Sobabili was not afraid. He
asked the lion, "Have you seen the
monster that ate my children and
ruined my home?"

"Do you mean the Mother of Monsters, the Crusher of Trees, who rose from the river baring her teeth, because of a princess who wouldn't say 'please'? Yes, she passed this way. Keep on going."

Sobabili thanked the lion and kept going.

At last, he saw a big,
dark hill ahead of him. But
then he saw that the hill had
a huge head. And the huge
head had bulging eyes and a
wide, greedy mouth.

41

He walked towards it and
asked, "O great one, have you seen
the monster that ate my children
and ruined my home?"

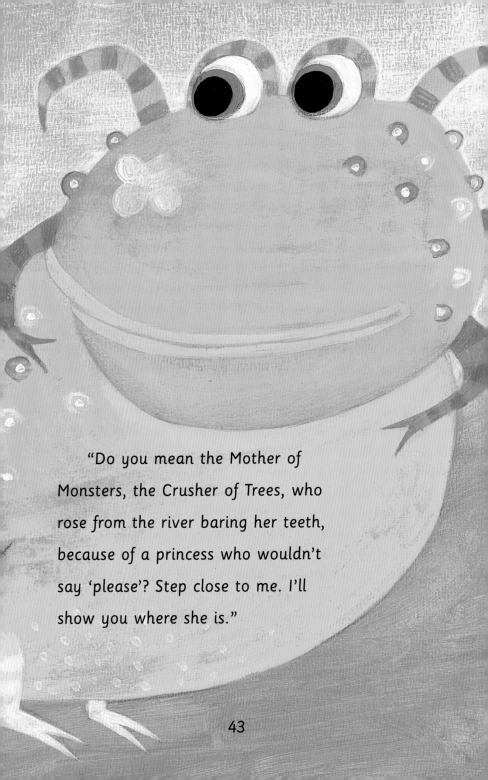

"Do you mean the Mother of
Monsters, the Crusher of Trees, who
rose from the river baring her teeth,
because of a princess who wouldn't
say 'please'? Step close to me. I'll
show you where she is."

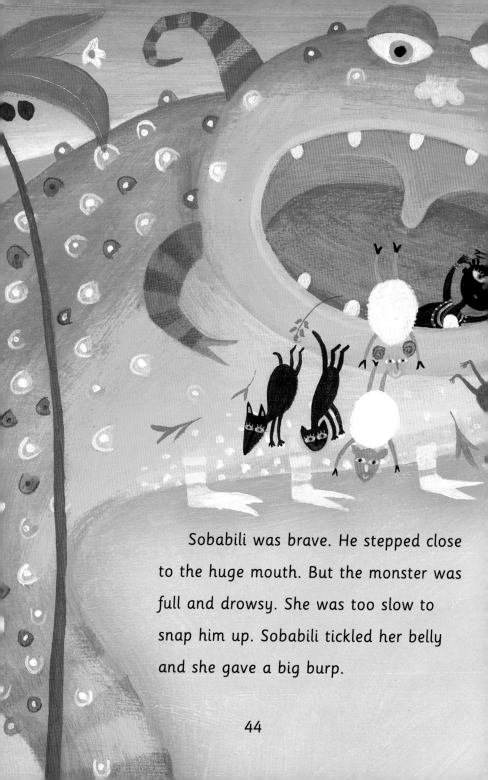

Sobabili was brave. He stepped close
to the huge mouth. But the monster was
full and drowsy. She was too slow to
snap him up. Sobabili tickled her belly
and she gave a big burp.

44

First, his two children tumbled out.
Then all the people, cattle and wild
animals that the monster had eaten
spilled out, including the nervous warriors.
Finally, the fearless princess plopped out.
They were all alive and well.

Ntombi was very sorry for causing so much trouble. "Please forgive me," she begged all the people that had been eaten by the Mother of Monsters.

At first, her father was very angry with her. But he could not stay angry for long. And when she told him that she would like to get married after all, he cheered up completely.

Sobabili was the first thing Ntombi had seen when she came out of the monster's mouth. She knew at once that she had found the man she wanted to marry. She had found a man without fear. She fell in love with him right away.

Ntombi and Sobabili were married and had a great wedding feast. They also had many more wild adventures together. The wilder the adventure, the happier they were!